Diary of an Enderman's Adventures

Book 2: Saving a Slime

Mark Mulle

TABLE OF CONTENTS

Diary of an Enderman's Adventure
Book Two: Saving a Slime

Day 1:

Hi! My name is Alton. I'm an Enderman, living in the End, and spending my days in the Overworld at work. We're trying to build an Overworld colony (but the key word is trying.) We don't make much progress with it. The teleporting thing is not something most Enderman can pull off, and it makes putting bricks in the same place at the same time something like a miracle. Yah! I know that's hard to believe but it's true.

I spend most of my time… looking for sweets to eat.

I have a best friend, Lydia, and she's a Slime.

I don't think I've seen any other Enders and Slimes working together.

Day 2:

While Lydia and I were venturing into the Redstone level of a cave, I saw something that nearly made me teleport away on accident: Obsidian stacked on top of each other, in some eerie purple glow. I know fully well what that means, and I tried to hurry back. But Lydia's mouth open so wide she could only take bounces half as big.

"The purple. Alton, it's… wow. Incredible." she stammered. Of all the words you could use to describe a portal to the Nether, incredible is not one of them.

I tried to pull her back, but it's hard

enough to yank her out of bouncing, let alone get a good grip. "You don't want to go there."

"What's behind it?"

"The Nether."

"Wow. Alton, isn't that where stones glow and lava comes out in lakes?"

"Trust me. You don't want to go there."

But she didn't want to talk about anything else for the rest of the night. I guess she wasn't the one who landed there on accident before and then wandered to the unknown side of the Overworld which happened to me. And I don't want her to be in that situation any time soon.

Day 3:

I took Lydia to the End today. My theory was this: if she saw something that's not Overworld, it will make her forget about her curiosity about the Nether and we won't have to mess with sarcastic Magma Cubes or creepy Ghasts (I know I'm a screeching black teleporter with purple eyes... but those Ghasts are terrifying.)

When we made it to the End portal tonight, my plan actually worked. She liked the constant darkness and thought the towers were beautiful, even the ones the End Dragon's already torn down. But then she simply had to see my own house. And, of course, Mom was in our hut, laying an end stone over some dirt a rather rude human left.

"So you're the slime?" said Mom, her purple eyes growing large. "What's it like in the Overworld? I haven't been there for a few Update Ages. You should come and have dinner with us at the End."

I shuddered. There's a reason I haven't invited Lydia to visit my house.

"I don't have anything happening tomorrow around midnight. Why not then?" Mom suggested it with such a calm tone that it almost felt like inviting other creatures to other parts of the Overworld is normal.

"Mom!" I shouted, but of course that

message didn't make it through her ears. I'm still not entirely sure where our ears are, anyway.

Lydia didn't help much, either. "Tomorrow at midnight?" she confirmed. "Sounds like a plan."

Entertaining something that's never seen this side of the world in front of a person who knows how to embarrass anyone is a "plan" all right. It looks like I have some damage control to do.

Day 4:

Mom is trying to make some "preparations" for Lydia's visit to the End in a few days. She thinks it would be "exciting" to play some games with some different mobs. She's planning on bringing out Sign-tionary.

Oh my! Not that game. Every time I try to draw something, it reminds her of some adorable thing I used to do as a kid. It's bad enough to re-live it by myself, but doing it with Lydia in tow will be torture. I'll asked Mom to tone it down, but who knows if she'll listen?

Mom has seen enough of slimes, zombies,

and spiders from her time trying to build in the Overworld to not stare, but she still doesn't know much about them. What if she starts asking questions like "What do you like to do in your free time?" or (ugh!) "Do you have any brothers and sisters?" Why do moms like to ask things, anyway?

Maybe I should give her a briefing about what I've learned so we can avoid the more awkward subjects. I guess the only way to learn is to ask, no matter how strange the question is. If there's anything I can do to make sure Lydia still wants to speak with me after this night, it's worth trying.

I'm not sure how the rest of the End will behave, either. It's so rare to see anything not yellow, black, or white on this side of the portal. Especially something that bounces so much. At this rate, I'll need to make a pamphlet or host some seminar for the whole colony.

Day 5:

If I can't prepare the whole End, the least I could do is prepare Lydia for our adventure. She's learning how to slow down as she speaks and sound less like she's stuck on top of a sticky piston in overdrive. Then again, that could be because I spend enough time with her that I can understand what she's saying easily.

I tried to warn her about Sign-tionary. But she says she's played a game like that before, guessing the word from a picture, and is looking forward to it.

Maybe I'll get lucky and think of something

really embarrassing Mom has done. Then I can blurt it out while she's drawing. Then again, can she draw, or will everything just look like triangles on top of each other?

Lydia's more excited than anything: "Everyone thinks their family must the strangest," she told me. "I'm sure this will be completely normal, Alton... except for the whole being in the End part."

At least she's distracted from the Nether portal- but I'm not entirely sure this is an improvement.

Day 6:

The dinner is not until tomorrow, so I have a chance to prepare the colony-building guys before the rumor mill starts. It's amazing how meeting someone green and slimy makes talking to creatures who look like you a little easier. There were really interested about Lydia. Especially since I told them about how we like to scare villagers into dropping things. Turns out I'm not the only person fascinated by Overworld stuff… though I'm still the only Ender who thinks cookies are better than week-long vacations.

The colony guys' biggest worry (besides

trying to put bricks on top of each other, which should be our biggest worry) is that she might break a few towers with her jumping. After all, we're not really well-known for our construction expertise. I'm worried that she's going to make a sticky mess. Maybe I can convince Mom to clean it up since this was her idea so even slime is not an issue.

Day 7:

Well, that was the most embarrassing evening of my life. And that's counting all the embarrassing experiences I had in the past that Mom mentioned to Lydia tonight. We actually had to put a box of dirt around her so she didn't break the door to our house. Inviting your friend over only to put her in a cage (for her own good, you still don't think any less of her) within ten minutes of the visit has to be a new record of some sort.

Mom still found a way to put a little sign in her cage so she could play the game with us, of course. And my carefully crafted pile of

Redstone (it's hard to draw red stone when you only have the color black, so I think I did an excellent job) reminded Mom, of course, of the outhouse incident.

She doesn't need to bring up the past like that. I was barely more than an Endermite when that happened. That outhouse was stinky, and the Overworld can be a little scary, and I just couldn't hold it anymore. Let it go, Mom, but not in the same way I let it go in front of the outhouse. (Okay, so I might have had an accident right outside the outhouse.) And for the love of all creatures great and small in the End, don't tell the story to Lydia.

After that, I broke down Lydia's box, and she hopped away without saying a word, heading back to the Overworld portal where she came. I don't want to see her leave, but at the same time I understand why she wanted to end the night before it hit rock bottom. I need to go find some sugar and punch the living daylights out of a rock.

Day 8:

I tried to stay in the colony and work. I actually carried some stone to our colony, laid it down, and came back.

But I had to know what happened to my first and closest friend. She wasn't in the village, which is where I somehow end up during the second half of the day. Every single day. It can't be that the Enders are easily distracted, of course. Speaking of which, have I told you about how unique the flavor of pumpkin pie is?

Never mind.

She wasn't in the caves, and as much as I

searched the fortress, I didn't see her. Did we honestly embarrass her off that much? I'll stay in the Fortress for now. Maybe if I keep my feet floating around her home, I can at least find some clues as to where she ran away.

I have a feeling in the pit of my pearl that tells me where she went. I just hope that I'm wrong.

Day 9:

I found her father. It's strange that I've never met him before. Maybe Lydia's family makes her shudder just like mine. But as far as I can tell, her dad has nothing to hide... except that things that don't move scare him a little. I've never seen a cock-eyed, suspicious bounce like that.

He says he hasn't seen her all day. He didn't seem too keen to meet me. I wonder if he thinks I'm the one who carted her away. But if she's not here, and she's not in the End, then that means... she must have wandered off into the Nether.

That would explain why she hasn't come back. Maybe Jason the Magma Cube found her and told her the story while still laughing over the time I fell through the portal on accident and he had to lead me out. That would be the best-case scenario.

It's the only lead I have, so I have no choice. Do they make fireproof armor that Endermen could use?

Day 10:

If I'm going back into that lava hole, the least I could do is go back prepared. I told some of my work friends why I wouldn't be helping them at the colony, and they promised to cover for me. It's a noble quest, not skipping work, so I don't feel too bad about it. But I don't want to scare all the little mites at home with one of the Dragon's rampages once he finds out I'm missing.

I let Mom know where I was going, too. She was worried when I didn't show up the last time I was lost in the Nether. She didn't want me to leave, naturally, but she also said she has never seen me this concern about a friend.

Day 11:

I would give anything for a visit from Jason.
Sure, I managed to narrow Lydia down to a
certain realm of the universe, but there are so
many places one Enderman can check,
especially with all the creepy mods glaring at
him. It seems like the farther I go, the longer
the Nether stretches, like the world is
building itself around me. It must be a nasty
trick of this place.

I did find a fortress. If Lydia was lost, it
would make sense that she would go to a
large place close to where she wandered into
the Nether. I'll stay here, and hopefully some

Ghast that keeps its screeching to a quiet, pleasant level will be able to give some clues. Yes, and maybe this Nether rock will feel just like Mom's obsidian couch that always smells like fresh flowers.

Day 12:

I saw a skeleton today, and since he was the only thing not actively trying to shoot me he was the perfect candidate for questions. But, naturally, he sprinted away, a giant sword huddled in between his ribs. He would hit himself on accident before he ever hit me.

In his hurrying, he did drop one extremely valuable slime ball. There's only one way he could have come across one of those precious things: Lydia is nearby. I tried to chase him down, but the skeleton decided to jump on top of some forsaken cliff.

Day 13:

I've been stuck in this black, sandy goo for half a day now, and I can't teleport out. It's like someone worked slime into the whole rock. And the worst thing about it is that I'm only a few blocks from a tiny cage that keeps popping out skeletons, all of which have the same reaction to me- they were all running for their lives. Am I that scary looking?

Day 14:

I did come across some skeletons today that did not find me scary. They definitely saw me, but I don't think they realized I could understand them. And I'm pretty sure they took "Have you seen a slime?" as some sort of dangerous code.

Does "Please help" translate to "I want to hurt you?"

"Let's put it in a cage and see what Boss has to say" one of them said. Forget baking. If I make it out of this corner of the Nether alive, I'm going into linguistics and learn the language of the other mobs.

Day 15:

I met their boss today. He made my boss look like a purple bat throwing an Endermite-size temper tantrum. At least the End Dragon only has one head to worry about. Half the time, I wasn't sure which head was trying to talk to me and which was barking orders at the skeletons.

He's convinced he's never seen a slime ball or a "green magma thing" in his life. And while at least one head trusted me, the other two were suspicious enough to leave me in this stone cell, "just in case you try anything." It's almost like I'm terrifying to these skeletons, just because they have never seen anything like me before. They live in one of the scariest places on Earth- how could they possibly fear me?

There's so many things we don't understand about each other. It's tragic what could be cleared up with just a little open and honest discussion between mobs. For one thing, it could save a scared little green slime from being lost and lonely and potentially hurt.

Day 16:

Jason finally came! I've never been so happy to hear from a laughing, sarcastic Magma cube. When I saw that bit of black bobbing from the top of the cage, I shook to my Ender Pearl. There must be something wrong with this Nether dust because it made this wet purple stuff come out of my eyes, too.

Jason was willing to bounce over to wherever part of this fortress the three-headed beast wants to call home and explain my situation and poor Lydia's potential disaster to the boss. The boss is curious enough to see what a green Magma Cube looks like to let me go.

He nearly pulled my arm, but the boss
yanked me out of the sludge, too.

The Magma Cube says that this vile stone
mush is called soul sand. I don't think the
sand has much of a heart or a soul. I'll give it
another name if I ever make it back home in
the End. "Stuck Sand" would be the least foul
one to use.

The good news is that Jason agreed to help
me on this quest… it was the least he could
do for the "poor little cage kid." And, of
course, he thinks all this is hilarious. I guess
laughter is a better response than
hyperventilation.

Day 17:

Our party has been sent on a noble quest: to save a damsel slime in distress in an unknown land. This reminds me of a game we used to play back in school where we saved our toys from the top of block towers. I guess this journey is sort of like being a knight. There was a dungeon involved, after all, but it wasn't nearly as fun as the ones we imagined.

We have followed rumors from the Nether-folk about a strange green cube from the top of a lava-fall about a week ago, and while I'm fairly certain she was here (it would make sense to look out from a high place when you're lost, and Lydia's pretty logical) there's no sign of where she went next. As frustrating as this is, at least I'm not a black rat in a cage anymore.

It took most of the day and what little teleporting skills I have to make it here, and we're both tired, so we decided to rest- wait, what was that rustling in the background?

Day 18:

I didn't want to write about it because I don't want to make myself panic (especially when Jason's here to bobble his head and snort at me), but there's no doubt that something was following us up the lava-fall. Every time I turned around, there was a bit of black that wasn't quite a shadow.

And now, it's come to light: A skeleton has been tailing us most of the day. When we saw him, he tried to run, but thankfully Jason was quick to cage him with bouncing.

There's no reason to lie to a diary, even if the thought wasn't flattering: I wanted to build a cage for him and walk away without explaining myself so he knew exactly how I felt. But Jason had more sense and used the soul sand to freeze the skeleton to one spot and give him a chance to explain himself.

His name is Jasper. He's a bit small for a skeleton, and his bones shiver when he talks. More importantly, he's had a conversation with Lydia and knows where she is. The Boss had given orders that none of the skeletons talk to us, and he was afraid we would attack him if he approached us directly. (And I guess we did sort of attack him.)
Jasper said that Lydia's been stuck on an island surrounded by lava.

Day 19:

Lydia's safe! She's alive and she's with us!
And she ate the cookie I saved for myself.

We found her stuck on an island in the
middle of a lava lake, and there was no way
she could jump to the mainland safely. I had
never seen her so tired and worn… and so
happy to see me.

Jasper said he saw her shortly after she
realized she was stuck, heard her cries for
help… and ran away. How was he supposed
to help, anyway? As much as I hate for Lydia
to be stuck like this, I know what it's like to
be scared. I'm still mad, but I'll come to a

point where I can forgive him for abandoning Lydia.

And to his credit, Jasper brought some rocks Lydia could hop on to reach the mainland and land into my black arms. She doesn't have arms like me, which is good, because if she could hug me as hard as I hugged her, she would have suffocated me.

Day 20:

Now that we have the easy part out of the way, the real fun begins: trying to find a way out of the Nether. With Jason's help, it shouldn't take us too long. But he's not really an expert on knowing where to go to leave his home; he's never even seen the Overworld. Maybe we can learn more about each other by seeing where everyone lives. I'll tell the End Dragon this trip was a research experiment.

At least Lydia has had a chance to explain herself amid all this wandering. She was embarrassed after our End outing and needed some time to chill. (We both agree on one thing: a place filled with fire and lava is not a great place to cool off.) She found the waterfall and was planning to see the top and then come home. But then she lost track of which block was under her and fell onto that blasted island. She's been a little shy since admitting all this, but if she can see past my obsession with cake, then I can look past this. Isn't that the whole point of friendship?

Day 21:

I wish we didn't have to leave Jasper in the Nether like that. I completely understand why he can't come with us- he's already breaking enough rules by joining our little quest- but I will miss hearing that pleasant rattling behind me when we move. After all, who knows where Lydia would be if it wasn't for him? He still seems a little scared of me and Lydia. I still don't know how he can look his boss full in the face without fainting.

Jasper left us a souvenir that I still don't quite understand: Soul Sand. Why he thought I wanted a memento of the thing that kept me locked for a full day is beyond me. But Lydia took it graciously and put it on the top of her head. She still says it was a nice gesture. She says we could use it as a trap, or maybe a memento of some sort. But why would we make something like that?

Day 22:

Wonderful. We've had such a lucky streak with the humans thus far that I thought we could make it back to the fortress and end this journey on a high note. But of course, we come right in the middle of a battle.

On the bright side, we were able to run while a band of killer bunnies attacked the poor human. He was so unprepared, even I'm willing to call him "poor": No armor, wooden sword, and out in the open.

Day 23:

Lydia's my best friend and all, but I wouldn't say no to putting her in another box so she doesn't make any more stupid decisions. "Let's make a little monument to Jasper, Alton," she says. "We'll probably never see him again, so we can tell other people about him," she added. But, of course, once we put the soul sand and the skull together… the Wither boss pops out of nowhere.

I don't know what we would do if we weren't within teleporting distance of the fortress and I actually managed to build a decent wall in a panic. This one didn't recognize us at all and didn't seem to remember anything about an Enderman saving a slime ball in the Nether. Not that I could talk much as he tried to demolish everything in sight. The sun is rising, so there are no skeletons or creepers or even those thick-headed zombies to come fight on our behalf. We are forced, once again, to sit and wait as we hear the growls of this beast. What I would give to have Jasper here instead of his "memorial tribute"!

Day 24:

Some of my colony-building friends showed up in this fortress. They say the past few days have been boring without me. I don't know whether to be thankful that they actually miss me or put my hands around that space in between their neck and body because I'm jealous that they can describe the past week as "boring".

They were thankful that I somehow survived all this… but not enough to take on the Wither boss themselves. We had to squeeze to make room for them in our little box; I barely have enough elbow room to write this down on paper. We've heard the boss's growls grew louder, quiet, then loud again- we have no idea when the coast will be clear. Lydia's restless. She spent the past week trapped on a fiery island only to be trapped behind a wall while a boss destroys her house. Not to mention her dad is somewhere in the pile of rubble growing around us. I've never seen her this mad. "We have to do something…" she mutters. "We have to do something…" and whenever I call her out on her muttering she's clearly still muttering in her head. I don't know what she's planning, and I am terrified I will find out.

Day 25:

Creepers.

Even an Enderman can't seem to coexist with creepers. Maybe I'll find out why one day. But first, I have to make sure Lydia stays alive.

As soon as one Creeper came near our fortress- as soon as we heard that horrendous hissing- Lydia gave an extra-large jump. The creeper crater was enough to take a few blocks out of our dirt walls, and before we could stop her she ran outside the fortress head-first. (I guess that isn't saying much considering she's all head... but you know what I mean.)

"For Slimes!" she yelled, and butted the boss. I was able to teleport to her before one of the three heads attacked, but all of the green has drained out of her face, and that can't be a good sign.

Since my Enderman friends aren't much help, and Lydia is in need of help herself, I see one person who might be able to take this monster. But I'm trapped- there's no way I can reach him and make sure Lydia stays safe.

Day 26:

My best friend is back! I know I've never actually met this human, but I don't care- if he can take on this boss and live, he'll earn the title of best friend. It looks like he's a bit better equipped than last time, but I'll give up every book I own if it means he could put some spells on his gear.

I broke a square in our little fortress, and as long as they stay on this side of the mountain I can root for the warrior. Though it looks like he's taking damage, and… he either fell into a ditch, or he will have to try again after he respawns. All of his stuff is gone, too. I feel his pain, but I feel the frustration of being stuck in this Creeper-blasted fortress, too.

What's more, he destroyed the portal to the Nether in the process, so any hope of reaching Jasper, even if it's a bunch of really lucky breaks strewn together, is lost. I'm sick of being stuck behind this dirt wall as much as Lydia was. We have no plan, no safety, and nothing to gain.

Day 27:

When the human fell to the Wither, he dropped a little cage. The only thing I could think of was "What an excellent surprise! More mobs to attack us!"

I have never been so happy to see a hostile mob in all my life. Popping out of the spawner, back shining against the small lake the boss had created via explosion… was Jasper! Even before he saw us, he wielded his little stone sword valiantly. Thankfully, the rubble is full of places to hide, and he even managed to make a few hits… until he fell out of sight a few minutes ago.

Is he alive? Is he injured? I'm sick of watching and waiting. There is only one course of action to take. I hope my teleportation skills still work.

Day 28:

There the Wither Boss was, all three heads glowing with glory, and gloating. They shook like they were laughing against the dark sky, daring even the moon to attack him. He reared back, preparing for the final blow to Jasper… then I teleported in front of him.

I was able to teleport behind him enough to confuse him, and once he lost his bearings Jasper managed a few punches before the Wither could react. And once he reacted, it was my job to teleport around his again until he was confused. It was a long, slow process with a few injuries to Jasper and me, but we were somehow able to pull it off. We used a fairly brilliant strategy, if I do say so myself, especially since Jasper and I figured it out as we went along and couldn't really pause to discuss logistics.

I might feel the lack of a right arm for a few days. Maybe even a few years. And Mom will have to stop giving me a hard time about being left-handed. But I wouldn't take any of it back. Together, we stopped the Wither Boss. No humans, no zombies, no creepers, just Jasper and me.

Strange. I thought that if something like this ever happened to me, I'd wonder if I got my own plaque. But I am too happy to be alive to care. I can barely move my left stub for all the soreness. And we need to tell Lydia's father that she is safe, as well as ask if I can still keep my colony-building job.

Day 29:

I've never seen the End Dragon smile before today. I've never seen a slime cry gooey green tears, either. And I don't think I'll ever be called "hero" that many times in one day again. It's a relief to have this mess behind me, enough of a relief that I can't wait to crawl into the village for a bit of cake.

I was given back my job at the colony.

Day 30:

Jasper comes to visit us in the village today with some news. It looks like we changed the way the Nether mobs see mobs from other places. They have learned, at least, that Enders are no more scary than they are, and if a mob comes by that's not recognizable, then talking to it is a little more effective than trying to hurt it. The Boss we made on accident was not the one we met in the Nether. The Boss was sorry that he initially prevented Jasper from helping Lydia, but he was so happy to know that Lydia is back safely to her fortress. Jasper might see us in the Overworld a bit more often now and I am so much thrilled with that.